TOUCHDOWN TRIUMPH

BY JAKE MADDOX

Text by Brandon Terrell
Illustrated by Aburtov

STONE ARCH BOOKS
a capstone imprint

Jake Maddox Sports Stories are published by Stone Arch Books
A Capstone Imprint
1710 Roe Crest Drive
North Mankato, Minnesota 56003
www.capstonepub.com

Library of Congress Cataloging-in-Publication Data
Maddox, Jake, author. Touchdown triumph / by Jake Maddox ; text by Brandon
Terrell ; illustrated by Aburtov.

 pages cm. -- (Jake Maddox sports stories)

Summary: Because his father is in the Army, Oliver Jeffries has never lived in any
one place for long, but he was hoping that Colorado would be different because he
is the starting wide receiver on Jackson Middle School's football team – so when
he gets word that his family is moving again he is bitterly disappointed, but he has
one more game and he is determined to make it a good one.

ISBN 978-1-4965-0492-0 (library binding) -- ISBN 978-1-4965-0496-8 (pbk.) --
ISBN 978-1-4965-2324-2 (ebook pdf) -- ISBN 978-1-4965-2466-9 (reflowable epub)

1. Football stories. 2. Moving, Household--Juvenile fiction. 3. Military dependents--
Juvenile fiction. 4. Middle schools--Juvenile fiction. 5. Families--
Colorado--Juvenile fiction. 6. Colorado--Juvenile fiction. [1. Football--Fiction. 2.
Moving, Household--Fiction. 3. Children of military personnel--Fiction. 4. Middle
schools--Fiction. 5. Schools--Fiction. 6. Family life--Colorado--Fiction. 7. Colorado-
-Fiction.] I. Terrell, Brandon, 1978- author. II. Aburto, Jesus, illustrator. III. Title. IV.
Series: Maddox, Jake. Impact books. Jake Maddox sports story.

PZ7.M25643To 2016
813.6--dc23
[Fic]

          2014043712

Art Director: Bob Lentz
Graphic Designer: Veronica Scott
Production Specialist: Katy LaVigne

Printed in the United States of America in Eau Claire, Wisconsin.
102015   009291R

TABLE OF CONTENTS

CHAPTER 1

ANOTHER NEW TOWN

Oliver Jeffries sat slumped in the backseat of his parents' car. His long, lean legs were propped up, knees pressing into the seat in front of him. A pair of headphones blasted bass-thumping hip-hop music that his mom often told him would "rattle a screw loose someday."

Oliver looked out the window just as the vehicle passed a large sign on the side of the road. It read: WELCOME TO JACKSON! HOME OF THE FIGHTING BULLDOGS!

Oliver sighed. *Another new house in another forgettable town,* he thought.

Oliver was no stranger to new towns. His dad was in the Army, which meant their family was often relocated. They had lived in six different places in the past four years. This time it was Jackson, Colorado. By now, Oliver was used to moving around, but that didn't mean he enjoyed it.

They drove through a nice neighborhood of two-story homes. Towering trees lined the streets, casting afternoon shadows on the lawns. They pulled up next to the curb in front of a yellow house with white trim. A red *FOR SALE* sign was posted in the front yard with a *SOLD* sign plastered over it.

Oliver clicked off his music. Even though it was silent now, his ears were still humming.

"Home sweet home," Mom said, opening her door.

"Again," Oliver added under his breath.

Next to him, Oliver's seven-year-old sister, Addie, was ready to burst. "I can't wait to pick out my bedroom!" she said, her nose pressed against the window.

"Knock yourself out," Oliver muttered as they all climbed out of the car and headed inside.

The empty house was more spacious than their last home. More wood floors and less carpeting. The last place they'd lived had had green-and-yellow patterned wallpaper in the kitchen — a color combination that had made Oliver want to puke. Thankfully, this kitchen was neither green nor yellow.

Addie ran around the house like she was on a treasure hunt. Finally, she happily cried, "I found it! I want this room!" Her words echoed through the empty house.

Dad stepped up behind Oliver and placed one of his massive hands on Oliver's shoulder. He wore a gray shirt that read ARMY in black letters across the chest. "The moving truck should be here later this afternoon with the rest of our things," he said.

"I guess I should find my new bedroom then, huh?" Oliver said. He shoved his hands into his sweatshirt pockets and began to walk away.

"Son?" Dad's voice, usually booming and loud, had softened.

Oliver turned around. "Yeah?"

"I know how much you dislike moving," Dad said, "but this time it's going to be different."

"Really?" Oliver asked.

Dad nodded. "Promise."

Oliver wanted more than anything for that to be true, but he wasn't sure he could believe it. After all, Oliver had been let down before, having to leave places he thought of as home.

"Now, what do you say we find the best place in town to get a meat lover's pizza?" Dad asked, a grin creeping across his face.

Oliver nodded. "Sounds good, Dad," he said. But as he wandered off to explore his new house, Oliver couldn't help but wonder just how long he would call this place home.

CHAPTER 2

FIRST DAY OF SCHOOL

The following Monday was Oliver's first day at Jackson Middle School. He knew the drill — head down, don't talk to anyone, don't draw attention to yourself.

He had been through the same experience many times. Because his family moved around so much, Oliver never really made friends. It just made it that much harder to say goodbye when he had to move again.

He thought about what his dad had told him the day they'd arrived in Jackson, about how this time would be different.

Maybe he's right, Oliver thought. *Maybe we'll be here for a while. It wouldn't be terrible. Jackson seems like an okay town so far.*

Oliver walked through the school halls, his head lowered, hands gripping the straps of his backpack. He found the glass door that led to the main office and walked inside. An older woman with wavy black hair and a kind smile sat behind a desk. Her nameplate read *Ms. March.*

A boy about Oliver's age, lean and muscular with close-cropped dark hair, sat in a metal chair against the wall.

"Good morning," Ms. March said. "You must be Oliver Jeffries."

"Yes, ma'am," Oliver replied.

"Welcome to Jackson Middle School, Oliver," she said as she plucked a blue folder from a pile on her desk. "This is your class schedule, as well as some information about our school programs. Fall sports are just getting underway, so there's still time to register." She handed Oliver the folder.

"Thank you," Oliver said quietly.

The boy who was seated in the office stood up then.

"Oliver, this is Andy Kingbird," Ms. March said. "He'll show you to your first class this morning."

Andy held out his hand. "Nice to meet you, Oliver," he said with a smile.

"You too," said Oliver, shaking his hand.

The two boys exited the office. The halls were beginning to swell with kids arriving for the day. Oliver and Andy joined the crowd.

"'Sup, Andy," a tall boy standing at his locker called. He was wearing a T-shirt with the words *Jackson Bulldogs Football* on the front. "Ready for practice today?"

"You know it, Tristan," Andy replied. The two boys bumped fists.

As they walked down the hall, Oliver noticed that many of the kids greeted Andy. He seemed quite popular.

They stopped at Oliver's locker before continuing on to his first class, which was geography. As they walked down the hall, Andy asked, "So, did you play football at your old school, Ollie?"

Oliver was surprised. People rarely called him Ollie. And certainly not people he had just met.

"Uh, yeah. At one of my schools," Oliver said.

"What position did you play?" Andy asked.

"Wide receiver," Oliver replied.

"Cool," Andy said with a nod. "I'm the Bulldogs' quarterback. You should sign up for the team. It's a no-cut sport."

"Maybe," Oliver said. "I'll think about it."

Normally, Oliver would have said no immediately. But Andy was a nice guy, and playing football again could be fun. It had been a while since Oliver had caught a pass, scored a touchdown, or heard the crowd cheering.

It had been forever since he'd felt like part of a team.

"Here you go," Andy said, stopping and pointing to a door. "Mr. Erickson's geography class."

"Thanks," Oliver said.

Once more, Andy offered his hand to Oliver. "I gotta get to Mr. Dahl's English class," Andy said. "See you around, Ollie. Maybe on the field?"

"Yeah," Ollie said, shaking his hand. "Maybe."

Then Andy dashed off down the hall, leaving Oliver on his own once more.

CHAPTER 3

PRACTICE

The next day, Oliver walked onto the football field, helmet in hand. He had given serious thought to Andy's suggestion to join the team the day before. After speaking with his parents about it, he'd decided to take a chance and sign up for the team.

"Ollie! You came!" Andy shouted. He threw his arms up in the air.

Oliver gave him a brief, nervous wave and walked toward a squat, muscular man who looked like he must be the coach.

The man was wearing a windbreaker, a ball cap, and a whistle around his neck, and he held a clipboard. Oliver was feeling uncomfortable. Since he hadn't played in a while, his shoulder pads were a bit too small. He wore an old pair of padded pants and cleats that felt tight around his toes.

"Hi, Coach," Oliver said, walking up to him. "I'm Oliver Jeffries. I just moved to Jackson, and I'd like to play for the Bulldogs."

"Welcome, Oliver! I'm Coach Barton," the man said. "I spoke with your dad last night. We're happy to have you join us."

Then Coach Barton blew his whistle and waved his arms at the team to bring it in. The team, including Oliver, circled up around him.

"We've got a new player joining us today," Coach Barton said. He looked across the circle at Oliver, who held up his hand shyly.

"How 'bout it, team?" Coach Barton said. "Let's give Oliver Jeffries a big Bulldogs' welcome."

In response, the team barked in unison three times.

"All right! Our season starts Friday, and we've got a lot of work to do," Coach said. "Let's have a good, strong practice! One, two, three . . ."

"Bulldogs!" the team shouted.

Andy led the offense onto the field, where they lined up to run plays. Oliver sat on the sideline and watched as the team ran through their playbook.

Whether he was handing the ball off to Tristan, the team's starting running back, or passing down the field to Chen Liu, one of the wide receivers, Andy seemed confident.

"Jeffries!" Coach Barton yelled. "Jump in at wide receiver and run a post route."

"Yes, sir!" Oliver called. He latched the chinstrap of his helmet and jogged onto the field. Taking his place, he let out a deep breath and waited for the snap.

"Hut hut!" Andy shouted. "Hut . . . hike!"

Oliver broke downfield, running as fast as he could. When he'd gone twenty yards, he cut right. He looked back over his shoulder. Andy had already thrown the ball. It was arcing right toward Oliver. He threw his hands forward and snatched the ball out of the air.

Coach Barton blew his whistle and started clapping. "Nicely done!" he shouted. "Let's see what else the new kid can do."

As Oliver jogged back to the line, Tristan said, "Sweet catch, Ollie."

Chen added, "Great footwork, man."

"Thanks, guys," Oliver said. Though he tried his best to stay cool, a grin crept across Oliver's face.

* * *

That night, after Oliver had showered and eaten, he sat on the floor of his room, surrounded by boxes. He never really unpacked when he moved to a new house. It just meant more work when his family had to move again.

Not this time, Oliver thought. He reached for the nearest box and cracked it open.

CHAPTER 4

GAME TIME!

That Friday, the Bulldogs had their first game at home against a team called the Henderson Gators. The wooden bleachers on either side of the field were packed with fans. As Oliver stood on the sideline, he spotted his parents and sister in the crowd. Addie waved wildly when she saw him.

The Bulldogs won the coin toss and took the kickoff. A surge of adrenaline coursed through Oliver's veins as he, Andy, and the rest of the offense took the field.

"Sweep left on three!" Andy called.

The players all lined up. Oliver and Chen's job on this play was to block for Tristan and give him a hole near the left sideline.

Andy pitched the ball to Tristan, who quickly darted up the field. A Gators' defender rushed toward him. Oliver lowered his shoulder and blocked the defender, giving Tristan room to run another fifteen yards.

"Nice block!" Tristan hollered. He slapped Oliver on the helmet as they jogged into the huddle together.

Next up was another running play up the middle and a quick pass to the team's tight end, a boy named Jonathan. It went off without a hitch.

Back in the huddle, Andy said, "Crossing route on three. I'm looking for you, Ollie."

Oliver sized up the defense. There was a large hole in the middle of the field. *Perfect,* he thought. *It'll be a breeze to cut in toward the middle for a crossing route.*

"Hut . . . hut! Hike!" Andy yelled.

Oliver cut across the field, his cleats chewing up grass. He saw Chen, who was mirroring his actions on the other side.

Chen and Oliver cut toward one another, and their shoulder pads were just inches from colliding. The defense was caught off guard, and Oliver found himself wide open. Andy zipped a bullet of a pass, and Oliver caught it and found the end zone easily.

The nearest referee threw his hands in the air and blew his whistle. "Touchdown!"

The crowd cheered wildly. A few fans even started barking like bulldogs.

The Bulldogs scored six points for the touchdown and one for the extra point. The score was now Bulldogs 7, Gators 0.

The Gators fought back, driving the ball forward before the Bulldogs' defense stopped them cold in their tracks. They were forced to kick a field goal, which earned them three points, bringing the score to 7–3.

Over the course of the game, Oliver caught several more passes, including a second touchdown. The Gators began to cover him with two of their defensive players, which left either Chen or Jonathan open. Andy took advantage of that and kept finding the open player.

By the time the final buzzer sounded, the Bulldogs had easily won by a score of 35–10.

CHAPTER 5

MAKING FRIENDS

Their win against the Gators was not by chance. The Bulldogs were a strong team, and over the next few weeks, they won three more games. Oliver had been playing really well and had scored at least one touchdown in each game.

The entire school was talking about the undefeated Bulldogs. Signs painted in the school colors — red and black — hung in the hallways. Some of them even had Oliver's name. They said things like, *#89 JEFFRIES 4 PRESIDENT!* and *TD OLLIE!*

Man, this is wild, Oliver thought as he walked through the halls one afternoon before practice. *Usually my classmates don't even know my name.*

But even with an undefeated record, the team knew they couldn't afford to get cocky.

The biggest challenge of the season was approaching. The Bulldogs were about to take on the Greenville Hurricanes, their biggest rival. Every year, the game between the two teams drew a lot of attention. The stands were sure to be filled. The Bulldogs were starting to feel the pressure.

That evening, after a tough practice, the Bulldogs trudged to the locker room in silence. As they dressed and gathered their things, Andy said, "We should do something fun. Relax a little. Who wants to go miniature golfing?"

"I'm in," Tristan said, shedding his shoulder pads.

"Let's do it," Chen agreed.

A handful of other players nodded in agreement. Oliver nodded too. *Why not?* he thought.

Putting Edge Miniature Golf wasn't far from school. After calling their parents to ask for permission, some of the guys rode their bikes over. Oliver walked there with a group, hanging toward the back of the crowd.

Once everyone arrived and paid, they were all given putters and multi-colored golf balls.

"Ollie! You're in our group!" Andy shouted, waving Oliver over to the first hole, where he, Tristan, and Chen waited.

Families and couples played on holes that featured windmills, pirate ships, and waterfalls.

Andy had been right. This was just what they needed. After working so hard, it felt great to get out and have fun.

With each hole, Oliver found himself laughing more and more. At one point, he and Chen began dueling with their putters, like two swordsmen engaged in battle.

The eighteenth hole was a large bulldog statue with a ramp leading to its mouth. The ball came out . . . the other end.

When it was Oliver's turn, Tristan said, "I bet ten bucks that Ollie can't sink his putt through the bulldog's mouth in just one shot."

Oliver laughed and said, "You're on."

Andy said, "All right, Ollie. Let's see what you've got."

Oliver stood over his ball. He swung the putter hard, knocking the ball up the ramp. It bounced off the bulldog's nose, sailing through the air and nearly hitting Andy, who ducked out of the way.

"Whoa!" he shouted. "Are you trying to knock me out, Ollie?"

The whole group burst out in laughter, and Oliver was beaming inside and out. *It feels great to have friends,* he thought.

The boys had finished their round of golf and were about to head their separate ways when Oliver said, "Hey! Who wants pizza?" He didn't want the fun to end just yet.

"Yeah," Andy said, clapping him on the shoulder. "Great idea, Ollie."

CHAPTER 6

BAD NEWS

Oliver was on cloud nine. He was also stuffed with pizza.

After hitting Gordon's Pizzeria, Oliver had split from the guys to walk home. The sun was setting, and the autumn temperature had dipped, making him shiver a little. Oliver didn't care, though. He couldn't believe how well things were going. His family was staying put. He'd made friends he enjoyed spending time with. And he was playing on an undefeated football team.

Everything was great.

But when Oliver stepped into his house, he could tell something was off. It was too quiet. He could hear Addie and his mom talking faintly. *They must be playing in Addie's room,* he thought.

His parents knew where he'd been, so Oliver knew he couldn't be in trouble. He had been sure to call and update them. And Mom had been chipper on the phone. "Enjoy yourself, sweetie," she had said. Oliver had been thankful his friends couldn't hear.

Oliver found his dad sitting at the kitchen table. When he spotted Oliver, Dad said, "Son, have a seat."

Oliver walked slowly toward the table, unsure what was going on.

"How was practice?" Dad asked.

Oliver shrugged. "Fine," he said, pulling the chair out and sliding into it.

Dad nodded. "Do you think you're ready for the game against Greenville?"

"Definitely," Oliver replied.

"Good." Dad paused and then said, "Oliver, I have some bad news."

Oliver's stomach flipped. He knew what his dad was going to say. He pushed back his chair, its legs scraping against the floor. "No," he said. "No way."

"I'm sorry," Dad said. "I've been relocated to Arizona."

It was like he'd been dunked in freezing cold water. Oliver clenched his fists. "But you said . . . no, you promised —"

"I know," Dad said calmly. "And I shouldn't have done that. I'm terribly sorry. But at the time, I thought it was true."

"When are we leaving?" Oliver asked.

Dad sighed. "Earlier than I expected. Later this month."

Oliver shook his head, unable to believe it. "This month? That's so soon."

"It is. Again, I'm sorry, Oliver," Dad said.

"Will I at least get to finish the football season?" Oliver demanded.

Dad's eyes answered for him, looking down at the table.

Oliver felt the sting of disappointment. "When's my last game?" he asked.

"The game against Greenville," Dad said. "I already spoke with Coach Barton."

Oliver stood up, knocking his chair onto the floor. "No!" he shouted. "You can't do this to me! I like it here! I have friends now!" Tears pooled in the corners of his eyes, blurring his vision.

Turning around, he saw his mother standing in the dining room doorway. When she'd gotten there, Oliver didn't know.

"Oliver . . ." Mom said. She started to walk over to give him a hug.

But Oliver backed away. "Just . . . just leave me alone!" He stomped over to the door, banged it open, and ran out into the cold, dark night.

CHAPTER 7

MEMORIES

Oliver ran.

He didn't know where he was going. He only knew that he needed to run.

His feet slapped against the sidewalk, and the brisk night air brushed against his tear-soaked cheeks. He should have seen it coming. He almost hated himself for not figuring it out. Things were going so well — too well. He'd let his guard down, and now he was hurt.

Again.

Oliver ran through his neighborhood and then cut through a huge city park lit by street lamps. Pools of yellow light flooded the park. His lungs burned. He could feel sweat dripping down his forehead and into his eyes, but he kept running.

Eventually, Oliver realized where he was heading. The school was up ahead, dark this time of night. He saw the football field draped in shadows and made his way toward the wooden bleachers, where he sat down to catch his breath. He used one sweatshirt sleeve to wipe the tears from his eyes. It was cold out, and he shivered.

On Friday night, just five days away, the bleachers would be packed with fans. Suddenly Oliver didn't know if he had the heart to play anymore. What was the point when he knew it would be his last game?

I won't get to finish the school year or even the season. Maybe I should just quit the team now, Oliver thought.

Just then, a pair of car headlights swept across the field from the nearby street. The car stopped, and the driver climbed out. For a brief second, Oliver worried that it was a policeman. But as the person walked closer, he realized that it was his dad.

Oliver said nothing as his dad sat down next to him. A long minute of silence passed before Dad asked, "Are you cold?"

"No," Oliver replied.

"Friday's game is going to be quite spectacular," Dad said. He gazed out at the field. "You and your friends are an amazing team. It's been a privilege to watch you play."

Oliver shook his head. He knew his dad was trying to make him feel better, but it wasn't helping. "Dad, are we always going to have to move around like this?" he asked.

Dad thought about it a moment. "No," he said. "Not always."

"Good," Oliver said. "Because I hate being the kid that everybody eventually forgets." At that, he broke down again, the tears coming easily.

Dad draped his arm around Oliver's shoulders. "Son," he said, "no matter where you are, you will always have the memories of what you accomplished. And I will always be proud of you. Friday's game? It's going to be memorable. I just know it." He stood up. "Come on. Let's go home."

Oliver followed his dad back to the car and climbed into the passenger's seat. He took one last look at the football field before his dad turned the car around and drove away.

CHAPTER 8

A TOUGH OPPONENT

That Friday night, Oliver sat in the locker room, suiting up for the big game against Greenville. Kickoff was less than an hour away. While the rest of the team told jokes or listened to music on their headphones, Oliver sat by himself. Ever since his dad had given him the bad news, he'd been avoiding his teammates.

"What's wrong, Ollie?" Andy asked, sitting down beside him. He was twirling a football in his hands.

Oliver shrugged. "Nothing."

"Liar," Andy said.

"Fine," Oliver admitted. "My family is moving again. This is my last game."

"Oh." Andy stopped tossing the ball, and his smile faded. "Sorry to hear that, man."

Oliver looked down. "Yeah. Me too."

Andy handed the football to Oliver. "Well, you should go out on top. Right?"

Oliver nodded.

"Then let's go out there and make your last game a win," said Andy.

* * *

"All right, Bulldogs! Let's show them whose doghouse this is!" Coach shouted as he paced along the sideline.

Oliver blew into his gloved hands to warm them. It was frigid outside. The weatherman on the news had predicted snow, but so far, only a few flakes had fluttered onto the field.

The Hurricanes won the coin toss and chose to kick off. On the first play, their receiver caught the ball and scurried to the thirty-yard line.

On the second play of the game, the Hurricanes' quarterback, a speedy kid named Avery, looked to pass. But then he ran up the field for more than twenty yards, crossing midfield easily. He had great instincts on the field and razor-sharp precision when he threw.

"Somebody tackle him!" Coach Barton shouted.

On the next play, the Bulldogs' defense tried to take out the Hurricanes' quarterback for a blitz. Avery was able to get the pass off before he was tackled, though, and the receiver dodged a Bulldogs' defender and ran into the end zone.

"Touchdown, Hurricanes!" the referee shouted.

The defense jogged off the field, shoulders slumped in disappointment.

"Don't get down on yourselves, team!" Coach Barton yelled. "There's a lot of game left!"

After the kickoff, Andy led the Bulldogs' offense onto the field. The snow was starting to come down harder now. It wasn't sticking to the grass yet, but it would be soon enough.

The first play from the line of scrimmage was a hand-off to Tristan. The running back drove forward, found a hole, and got a first down, advancing the ball ten yards.

"Great job!" Oliver said, clapping Tristan on the shoulder.

The Bulldogs decided to stay with the running game, attempting to drive the ball forward rather than pass it. Then, when the Hurricanes' defense expected Tristan to run the ball once more, Andy threw a perfect pass to Chen instead, who ran the ball into the end zone for a touchdown.

The Bulldogs tied the game at seven after getting the extra point. The crowd went wild.

After a field goal by the Hurricanes, the Bulldogs found themselves down again — this time by three points.

The Bulldogs were inside the thirty-yard line now, but time was running out, and the snow was starting to fall faster. It was becoming more difficult to see.

"We have one more shot at the end zone before time runs out," Andy said. "Post route on two. Break!"

Oliver lined up, waiting for the snap, then bolted down the sideline. He looked up, saw the last second tick off the clock, and cut toward the middle of the end zone for the post route. He was wide open.

Andy threw a beautiful spiral, and Oliver reached up . . . but the ball fell through his hands and bounced off the ground.

The crowd let out a collective sigh.

"That's the end of the first half!" the referee shouted, blowing his whistle.

CHAPTER 9

ONE LAST SHOT

At the start of the second half, the Bulldogs were still down 10–7. Snow had blanketed the field in white. The yard markers were difficult to see, and it was almost impossible to hold onto the ball.

On the first play of the half, Andy threw a pass downfield to Jonathan, the tight end. Jonathan fumbled, losing control of the ball.

A Hurricanes' linebacker quickly recovered the ball and then ran with it to the three-yard line.

On the next play, Avery flipped the ball to his team's running back, who danced into the end zone.

"Come on, guys!" Andy shouted from the sideline, trying to encourage the players. "We can do this!"

The score remained 17–7 through much of the second half. Players stumbled and slid across the field, and several passes were dropped. Each team fumbled once.

Still down by ten points, the Bulldogs' offense took the field.

"It's now or never!" Andy shouted. "We need a touchdown!"

On the first play, the snap was low and slipped from Andy's fingers. Still, he managed to scoop it up and run for fifteen yards.

Tristan tore down the field on the next play, and Chen contributed a thirty-yard catch on a crossing pattern. Then Tristan ran toward the sidelines and, with the help of Oliver and Chen's blocking, dove into the end zone.

"Touchdown!" the referee called.

After they got the extra point, there was only a minute left on the clock. The score was now Hurricanes 17, Bulldogs 14.

The Hurricanes brought the ball up the field, trying to run out the clock. After each play, the Bulldogs used a time-out. Their defense finally stopped the Hurricanes just shy of the forty-yard line. The other team was forced to punt.

"Great work, defense!" Coach Barton barked.

The Bulldogs caught a break when the punter slipped in the snow. His wobbly kick dribbled to midfield, where a Bulldogs' player jumped on top of it.

With only twenty-four seconds left now, Andy spoke up. "Out route on two," he said. "Make sure to get out of bounds so we can stop the clock. We're almost in field goal range. We can tie this and send it to overtime."

Andy took the snap, and Oliver broke for the sidelines. The pass hit his chest right in the numbers. He caught it and ran forward until he was tackled by a Hurricanes' player.

"The clock's still going!" Coach shouted.

Oliver scrambled to his feet and dashed back to the line. Andy took the snap and spiked the ball, throwing it at the ground to stop the clock.

The Bulldogs immediately huddled up.

Andy glanced up at the clock. "Six seconds left," he said. "Let's make this play count, guys. Post route on two. Break!"

The Bulldogs came up to the line. Andy yelled, "Hut . . . hike!"

Andy took the snap, and Oliver ran faster than he'd ever run before. His cleats slipped, but he didn't fall. As he turned to the middle of the field, he glanced over his shoulder. The ball soared through the air in slow motion. Defenders swarmed Oliver as he reached up and tried to snatch the ball.

It fell through his fingers.

Not again! Oliver thought desperately.

But the ball did not hit the ground. It landed in the hands of a Hurricanes' safety, who was so surprised that he bobbled it.

Oliver grabbed at it, and the ball fell toward the snowy field.

Just then another defender stumbled on the slick grass and fell down. Like a pinball, the football struck the fallen player's helmet and flipped back into the air — right into Oliver's hands. He held the ball, staggered forward, and dove across the goal line.

"Touchdown!"

The crowd roared as Oliver leaped to his feet. He held the ball up high. The rest of Oliver's team rushed the field as the clock ran down to zero. The Bulldogs had won 20–17. The snow was still falling hard, blanketing the field in white. But even that didn't stop the Bulldogs' celebration.

CHAPTER 10

THE FINAL GAME

"That's the last of it!" Dad said.

A full week had passed since Oliver and the Bulldogs had defeated the Hurricanes. The team's next game wasn't until the following Friday. By then, Oliver would be in his family's new home in Arizona.

The house was now as empty as it had been the day they'd arrived. Oliver stood in the living room with his parents as Addie ran through the halls, laughing and shouting, "My voice echoes. Echo! Echo!"

"All right. Let's ship out," Dad said.

"Give me a minute," Oliver said. Then he wandered down the hall and into his old bedroom. There was still one thing in there. Something he'd been too sad to pack up.

Taped to one of the bare walls was a newspaper article about the Bulldogs' win over Greenville. It featured a photo of the team. Oliver stood in the middle of the group, holding the game-winning ball.

Oliver peeled the article from the wall, folded it, and slid it into his pocket. As he walked, head down, out the front door, he heard a voice say, "What's up, Ollie?"

Oliver snapped his head up. Andy stood in the driveway, a football tucked under his arm. Behind him were about a dozen other Bulldogs, including Tristan and Chen.

"What are you guys doing here?" Oliver asked.

Andy tossed him the ball. "Coach gave us the afternoon off. We thought we'd get in one last game with you before you leave. What do you say?"

Oliver looked over to his parents and sister, who stood watching from the front curb, where their SUV was parked.

Dad smiled. "Go on. We've got time."

Oliver grinned. "Let's do it. Go Bulldogs!" His friends responded with three loud barks.

They split into two groups and lined up in the snowy yard. They tossed the ball, laughing and shoving each other into snow banks, not keeping score but not caring at all.

It was the most memorable game of Oliver's life.

AUTHOR BIO

Brandon Terrell is the author of numerous children's books, including several volumes in both the Tony Hawk 900 Revolution series and the Tony Hawk Live 2 Skate series, graphic novels for Sports Illustrated Kids, chapter books, and a picture book about trains. When not hunched over his laptop writing, Brandon enjoys watching movies and television, reading, watching (and playing!) baseball, and spending time with his wife and two children in Minnesota.

ILLUSTRATOR BIO

Aburtov has worked as a colorist for Marvel, DC, IDW, and Dark Horse and as an illustrator for Stone Arch Books. He lives in Monterrey, Mexico, with his lovely wife, Alba, and his crazy children, Ilka, Mila, and Aleph.

GLOSSARY

collective (kuh-LEK-tiv) — done or shared by a group of people

featured (FEE-churd) — included as an important part of something

forgettable (for-GET-uh-buhl) — not worth remembering

immediately (i-MEE-dee-it-lee) — right away

instincts (IN-stingkts) — behavior that is natural rather than learned

memorable (MEM-ur-uh-buhl) — worth remembering

privilege (PRIV-uh-lij) — a special right or advantage given to a person or a group of people

relocated (ri-LOH-kay-tid) — moved to a new place

spacious (SPAY-shuhs) — large and roomy; having plenty of space

undefeated (uhn-di-FEE-tid) — never having lost

unison (YOO-nuh-suhn) — saying or doing something together

DISCUSSION QUESTIONS

1. Oliver often feels out of place because his family has moved around so much. Have you ever felt out of place? Talk about how you dealt with the situation.

2. When Oliver's dad tells him they will have to move again, Oliver is angry, sad, frustrated, and upset. Talk about how you would have felt if you were in his position.

3. Do you think it was a good idea for Oliver to run away from home after hearing the news of the move? Discuss some other ways he could have reacted.

WRITING PROMPTS

1. Oliver makes some good friends in Jackson, despite having lived there for a short amount of time. Imagine you are one of Oliver's friends in Jackson. Write him a letter at his new address a couple of weeks after the move.

2. Since the Jeffries family is moving almost right away, Oliver has to stop playing with the Bulldogs in the middle of the football season. Write a paragraph about a time when you had to give something up before you were ready.

3. Do you think it was worth it for Oliver to be on the Bulldogs' football team, even though it was only for a few weeks? Explain your opinion in one or two paragraphs.

FOOTBALL DICTIONARY

- **blitz** — a rush of the passer by a defensive player

- **crossing pattern** — a play designed for the receiver to beat his defender by running across the field

- **down** — one of a series of four attempts to advance the ball ten yards

- **end zone** — the area beyond the goal line at each end of the football field

- **field goal** — a score of three points made by successfully kicking the football between the goal posts

- **fumble** — when a player who has control of the ball loses it before being tackled or scoring

- **out route** — a play in which the receiver cuts hard toward the sideline

- **possession** — an instance of having control of the ball

- **post route** — a play in which the receiver runs 10–20 yards from the line of scrimmage straight down the field, then cuts toward the middle

- **quarterback** — a player who leads a team's attempts to score, usually by passing the ball to other players

- **running back** — a player who carries the football on running plays

- **tackle** — to force the player holding the ball to fall to the ground

- **tight end** — an offensive end who plays on the line of scrimmage and can both block and catch passes

- **touchdown** — a score that is made by getting the ball over the opponent's goal line, either by running or passing

- **wide receiver** — a player who specializes in catching forward passes on offense

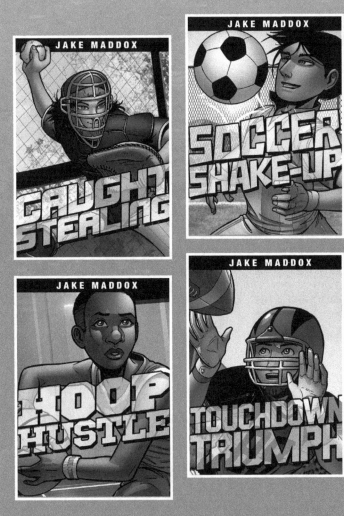

READ THEM ALL!